Silver Valley Witch

By

Annie Seaton

Silver Valley - Book 1

ISBN 978-0-6483990-7-0

Dedication

To my lifelong friends, Sharyn and Wendy…and to the memory of Helen, the inspiration for my culinary ghost.

Chapter 1

"A wager for you, my son." Venus leaned back, closing her eyes as she slipped a deep purple grape into her mouth. "I have found a woman you cannot entice to love."

Cupid leaned back in the soft cloud and snickered. "You have purple juice on your breast, mother."

"Damnation," Venus leaned forward, dangling bare legs in the azure blue of the soft air, scrubbing at the damp spot on her white flowing gown.

"Pray tell," replied Cupid, his voice bored. "I could do with some entertainment."

Venus laughed. "A worthwhile wager, my lad. Ten days on a tropical island in human form, with the man or woman of your choosing, if you bring this young woman to love." Cupid plucked at the strings of his bow and did not look at his mother reclining on the soft misty cloud.

"Mmm, how complete?" The young man with the cherubic face licked his lips as he thought of the reward.

"All the way…vows must be pledged." Venus smiled, languidly popping another fat grape between her lips, taking care not to let the juice trickle past her lips.

"Why such a good wager?" Cupid pointed his golden bow into the heavens and sweet music echoed off the cloud beside them as an arrow soared upwards.

"Because she is prudish and it will be an impossible task for you." A tinkling laugh followed the music into the clouds.

"Mother, you underestimate my power. A little arrow in the neck, zing and she will fall in love with the first man she sees."

"Follow me." A secret smile and Venus disappeared.

"Here we go again," sighed Cupid as he drifted through the clouds down to the human world.

***

"Excuse me." A languid voice interrupted Lizzy's filing and she cursed under her breath as the pile of cards fell over the front of the high library desk. A warm flush rose from her neck to her face as she stepped down from the high stool. As she walked around the desk, her elbow knocked a container of pens onto the floor, clattering down in the quiet of the library to join the cards at the feet of the two customers. Dropping her head down without looking at the owner of the bored voice, Lizzy attempted to conceal the blush spreading up from her neck, letting the strands of her silver blond hair swing across her cheeks

"I'm so sorry, I will be with you in a moment." She knelt to retrieve the square cards and pens that seem to have multiplied on their way to the floor. They were scattered around two pairs of shoes, a pair of white stilettos and a child size pair of white sneakers. As she scrabbled around on the floor, the little boy spoke, his voice surprisingly cultured.

"Really mother, this will be easy, although... a librarian?"

Lizzy's gaze travelled up two sets of legs, one clad in white trousers and the other in white lace stockings. Two very amused expressions met her gaze and her blush deepened as she realised the owner of the cultured voice was not a child but a little man. Fair skinned and light haired, the couple were both clothed completely in white. Lizzy could not take her eyes from the woman's face, she was the most beautiful person she had ever seen.

Realising she was staring rudely, she closed her mouth and scurried around to the safety of her desk, schooling her face into a professional expression. Placing the cards in a neat pile, she carefully put the pens into their container, as she gathered her composure.

"How can I help you?" she smiled at the couple waiting on the other side of the counter.

"Where are your sex books?" The strange little man may as well have been asking for cooking books, his expression was so bored.

8

ANNIE SEATON

"Ah, that would depend on…er …exactly what you are looking for?" Lizzy was determined to remain unperturbed. She had not seen this couple in the library before, and although the occasional tourist used the library services, it was generally to research family history or the many ghosts in the old buildings in Silverton. She rattled off some Dewey Decimal numbers.

"Biology is at five hundred and seventy four over to your left, sex roles are at three zero five point three and sex psychology at one fifty five point three, over to…"

"No, no, no," the strange little man with the cultured voice spoke loudly and heads turned from every corner of the small building. "We want a book about sex." He spelled it out as though she was simple. " S…E…X. Different positions and the like, perhaps you have a copy of the Kama Sutra?"

Lizzy fought the blush creeping up her neck. Picking up a brochure from the desk, she fanned her hot cheeks, as the little man gave a sly grin to the woman observing the conversation with a strange smile. Lizzy looked from one to the other, she was sure the little man had called the woman his mother, but she must have been mistaken. They were of a similar age.

"In that case, you will need to go over to the right, to six hundred and thirteen point nine." She gestured to the side of the library housing the nonfiction books. "I will be closing for noon break in five minutes, but I will reopen at two o'clock if you would like to come back then and join the library?"

"Would you get the book for me, now?" The little man persisted, arms folded across his chest. Feeling awkward and clumsy, Lizzy walked through the reference section, the couple close behind her, and she waved her hand at a mosquito buzzing past her head.

"Ouch," she slapped at her neck as it landed and bit her soft skin.

Reaching the end of the nonfiction shelves, she retrieved the Kama Sutra from the top shelf, and turned to the little man. They were gone. She stepped around the shelves looking around the library however they were nowhere to be seen which was most peculiar, as she hadn't heard the door open. Absently scratching at her neck, Lizzy shrugged her shoulders, as she crossed to the door to turn the Closed for Lunch sign and usher the remaining customers out. She sighed as a tall unshaven man pushed the door open, almost knocking her over.

"I need a computer."

She was going to be late for lunch.

***

Joshua Deegan ran his hand through his shaggy hair in frustration as he glared at the dowdy librarian blocking his entry. He was at his wits end. Three sleepless nights in an old farmhouse without air conditioning and wireless connection, and he was in a very bad mood. All he wanted was an internet connection. The librarian was staring at him, eyes wide and mouth open. Although, as he returned her startled gaze, he noted she was not as dowdy as his first quick look suggested, and he returned for a second appreciative glance. It was the brown homespun cardigan and the plain skirt hiding the shapely body that had formed his first impression.

11

Silver hair streamed past flawless skin, broken only by two spots of red, high on sharply defined cheekbones. Her silver-grey eyes reminded him of those of the rabbit caught in the headlights in the rutted driveway to the farm as his car had bumped down through the potholes on Friday night. Freckles lightly dusted a long narrow nose and broke the perfection of her skin. Lush, kissable lips formed a perfect O, as she continued to gape at him. She looked as if she was poised to run if he made a sudden move.

"Yes," he sighed, quite used to the effect he had on women. "I am Josh Deegan. Yes, you can have my autograph, I will even give you a signed copy of my latest CD… if you let me use a computer."

"Who?" The librarian hadn't moved and still gaped at him, as the blush spread across her face and neck.

"Josh Deegan, country and western singer." It was bad enough he had come to the wilds of Fairfield County, Connecticut to claim his inheritance. It was galling he had to spend the summer stuck in Aunt Helen's rambling farmhouse, and now he had struck the village idiot in the Silverton County Library. All he wanted was an internet connection.

When Aunt Helen's attorney read the will and told him of his windfall, the relief was tremendous, despite the codicil that he had to live at the farm for three months. Music sales had slowed with the global financial crisis, and his creativity had dried up. He would sell the property and inject some cash into the business at the end of summer. He'd be damned if he let a ghost he didn't even believe in, wreck his chance of reviving his career. It was an ideal time to write a new album.

"We're closed for lunch." Well, at least she could speak.

"What?" Josh glared at her. "Look, Miss…"

"Lizzy Sweet," she replied.

"Miss Sweet, I really need the internet. It appears this is the only connected place in town, there is not even WiFi anywhere, and it will take me three hours to drive out of this godforsaken valley to another town." He

13

could hear his voice rising along with his temper.

She continued to stare at him and Josh felt as though he was under a microscope. "We open at two o'clock, you are quite welcome to come in then and book a time on the computer." Her hands gripped the side of the door, her knuckles white.

"Book a time?"

"Yes," she replied quietly." I believe there is a free spot just before five o'clock. I will book you in then if you still wish to use the computer, Mr. Deegan."

"Yes, please, that would be wonderful, Miss Sweet." He did not hold back on the sarcasm. She nodded and turned the closed sign as he stalked down the library steps.

Chapter 2

Wesley watched Lizzy run gracefully across the road, dodging the lunchtime traffic. She was looking particularly dowdy today, and he grinned at her attempt to camouflage her shapely body in what appeared to be a brown sack. Old Mr. McGinty hooted his horn as he drove sedately past the town square, and Lizzy waited on the kerb for the old man to reverse the farm truck into a parking space, bumping vehicles front and back in the process. Wesley shook his head and waited for her as she helped the old man and his wife down out of the high cab of the truck.

"Honestly, Lizzy, how many old folk are on your daily help list?"

Flopping on the wooden bench next to her best friend and local warlock, Wesley Gordon, Lizzy ignored his gentle ribbing. He leaned in, inhaling the citrus fragrance of her silver hair, and lightly kissed her cheek. As his lips slid close to her mouth, she bumped him away with her shoulder, frowning at him. He reached over and pulled at her cardigan.

"Have you been shopping at the thrift store again?" Pushing his hand away, she ignored his comment.

"If you gave a bit back to the local folk, I wouldn't be constantly bailing you out of trouble, young man." Lizzy opened the lunch bag and handed him a sandwich wrapped in old-fashioned greased paper.

"Yum, lamb and mint jelly on pita bread. Thank you, Mrs. Macpherson." Wesley licked his lips.

The silence was companionable and Wesley reached for another sandwich as Lizzy sipped the brewed coffee he brought her each day.

"You're quiet today. Everything okay in your world?" Wesley's other hand landed on her knee and crept along her thigh. Wesley had fallen in love with Lizzy the instant he moved to the valley, delighted to find another of his kind in the quaint little town. Lizzy spent her time saving him from a variety of scrapes, unbelieving of his constant

16

professions of his love for her. Lizzy laughed, removing his hand from her leg.

"Just a peculiar morning, Wes. It's left me feeling a bit strange."

She scratched at her neck. Wesley's protective instinct kicked in. "If somebody has upset you…"

Lizzy interrupted him before he could get going. She always spoiled his fun, his lack of success with the most simple spells was a source of great amusement to her.

"I met a man," she said softly.

"What sort of man?" His stomach dropped as Lizzy looked at him, a faraway dreamy look in her eyes. Now he really started to worry, he had never seen that look on her face before. In fact, he had been trying to get her to look at him like that for a very long time.

Wesley had been in love with Lizzy for many years and his love remained unrequited, and he vowed to himself that he would not give up. He knew in his heart that Lizzy did really love him, she just had to realise that. Or that's what he told himself each day. They had

17

plenty of time. He was the only man who knew of her Wiccan world, and why she would never fall in love with a mortal man.

Lizzy was old. Really old. Over three hundred years old.

A survivor of the Salem witch trials in 1692, Lizzy carried a curse from those terrible days. As the witches burned, silhouetted against the black sky, orange smoke swirling from the pyre, an old crone had screamed a terrible curse at the young witches hiding in the crowd.

"I deny you love. If you take the love of a man for life, you will fall from immortality."

Over three hundred years later, Lizzy was the only witch left, the other young witches choosing love with a mortal man, over immortality. She abided by the Rede, the rule of conduct that said a witch may engage in any action, as long as it is carefully considered, and their actions harm nobody, including themselves. She also tried to get Wesley to follow the Rede, with no success.

"You're no fun, Lizzy, life is all about fun and good times." He complained each time she chastised him for breaking the code when he first moved to Silverton,

Over the centuries, her adherence to the Threefold Law ensured each of her actions came back to her threefold. Wesley knew Lizzy lived a good life, assisting many with her kind words and actions, living happily, if alone, in her little cottage on the edge of Silverton Valley. Over the years, she occasionally she worked a job for interest, but mostly sold her herbs and potions, along with a bit of ghost hunting. Wesley tagged along, and tried to make himself a vital part of her existence. She enjoyed his company, and he was her best friend, he had no doubt of that. Why now, in the twenty first century did a mortal man draw her attention for the first time? He watched as she rubbed at her neck.

"It's almost as though I have been charmed." Turning to Wesley, she narrowed her eyes and regarded him suspiciously.

"You haven't done anything foolish, have you?"

He put his hands up innocently.

"Like what?" He was most offended.

"Spells and potions?"

Wesley held up two manicured fingers. "Scouts' honour." I promised you, didn't I?"

Lizzy sighed and Wesley felt guilty even though he hadn't done anything. In the early days when he first moved to Silverton, Lizzy had rescued him from many scrapes, most often caused by inappropriate sexual liaisons. Under her strict instruction, he avoided spells, only dabbling occasionally in predestination at the county markets. He looked back at her, troubled by her sigh. It was out of character for her to be sad.

"There really is something wrong, isn't there, Lizzy. Let me look."

"No! You know how I feel about that." Wesley's true gift was the sight. Over the years, he had begged to look into their future and Lizzy fought him ferociously. "What would then be the point of living? We are immortal. Life would be pointless if we knew what lay ahead."

Lizzy finished her sandwich, leaned over and kissed his cheek.

"I'm okay, Wes. Promise me you won't look?" He put his arms around her, resting his chin on the top of her head.

"I would die of loneliness here without you Lizzy. I won't look. I promise." He spoke softly as he looked across the green grass to the ducks paddling in the millpond. "You know I do love you, don't you?"

She pulled out of his arms and bumped his shoulder again as she laughed up at him.

"No, Wesley, you just think you do, because I keep you out of trouble."

"Toss you for the last sandwich." He bumped her back.

"It's all yours, I have some chores to run before I go back to work."

"What poor old soul is in need of your ministrations now? " He wagged his finger at her, as she packed up the lunch papers. "And tell Mrs. Macpherson, they were the best sandwiches this week."

"You tell her yourself, when you mow her grass this afternoon. If you followed the

21

Rede, young man, I would not be constantly bailing you out of trouble. Wesley watched Lizzy as she strolled back along the path to the road, a deep unease settling in his stomach.

***

The afternoon passed quickly, the library was busier than usual. The regular customers were in. Old Mr. McGinty picked up his cowboy books and his wife took an armful of romances home in her voluminous flowered handbag. Two teenagers burst in after school seeking help with their overdue homework. The sole computer was in constant use. Looking down at the next name on the booking sheet on the front counter, Lizzy tried to ignore the butterflies in her stomach. She smiled as she shelved the Kama Sutra, the strange white couple had not come back in.

Lizzy's heart rate picked up as she heard the library door swing open half an hour before close. She sat quietly with her hands folded loosely on the desk, so she would not knock anything over in her usual clumsy fashion. A well-dressed, clean-shaven Josh Deegan walked over to the counter, cowboy boots clicking on the wooden floor, an open checked shirt revealing a long tanned throat. He produced a small bunch of miniature yellow roses from behind his back, holding them out to her with a sheepish expression on his face.

She peered at him over the top of her glasses, feeling the unfamiliar warmth start at her toes and work its way up her legs, her heart thudding and hands shaking. She now knew exactly whom Joshua Deegan was, even if unimpressed by the type of music he created. She had cared for his Aunt Helen before she passed on and had listened to many stories about her favorite nephew, but Lizzy did not intend pandering to his ego even though she was so strangely attracted to him.

"He lives in Nashville now and lives the life of a rock star," Aunt Helen had sighed. "He just needs the love of a good woman." Lizzy smothered a smile. All of her old friends in the valley were romantics, trying to marry her off to a variety of grandsons, nephews and family friends, but mainly to Wesley. Her own family had been pushing her at Wesley ever since they met him, that first year he moved to the valley. She was quite happy with the way she lived, thank you very much, and did not intend settling down with anyone. This attraction to Josh Deegan, country and western singer was bizarre.

"An apology for my extreme rudeness this morning," his deep voice sent the warmth spreading to her stomach. She reached out, willing her hand to stop shaking as she took the roses and buried her face in the perfumed petals. If she had known, the day was going to turn out like this, she would have worn something half-decent to work.

"You were a bit rude," she smiled. "But such a lovely apology is accepted." He brushed a finger lightly over the hand clutching the roses, and a quiver ran through her. It was crazy. All he had done was touch her, and she was trembling like a mould of jelly.

She stood carefully, ensuring anything able to fall off the desk was secure, leading him over to the computer on the back wall of the library, waiting until he sat. He looked at her without speaking. She returned his intense gaze, feeling uncomfortable as he stared her and she racked her brains for a witty comment. She finally cleared her throat, asking timidly,

"Is there anything I can help you with?" After all she was the librarian.

"No, thank you, not unless you have supernatural powers."

Feeling the warmth move to her face and neck, she hurriedly reached over him and typed in the pass code.

"Sorry, can't help there," she said nervously. "You have half an hour until close." She hurried back to her desk, knocking a book of the trolley on the way past. Looking back, she was relieved to see he hadn't noticed her clumsiness. What on earth was wrong with her today?

***

Josh spent the half hour checking his email, tweeting and adding an entry to his private face book page, so his friends knew where to find him. His cynical message advising them of the lack of phone service made him laugh. He couldn't even use his phone to access the web. As he googled a ghost search, he felt a quick tap on his shoulder. Embarrassed to be caught looking up ghosts, he closed the browser.

"Time's up, I'm about to close, Mr. Deegan." He looked up to a nervous smile on her pretty face framed by that swinging silvery hair.

"Ten more minutes? Can I bribe you with more roses…champagne…dinner?"

"I would love to, but we have to leave. The alarms are set automatically in the county office, for fifteen minutes after closing time. It just gives me enough time to lock the door and get out."

Running his fingers through his hair in frustration, he tried to keep his temper. Lack of sleep had played havoc with his mood over the past couple of days. It wasn't her fault he

26

had landed in Hicksville, courtesy of Aunt Helen.

"No problem, have I got time to borrow a couple of books?"

Nodding, she pointed at the antiquated card catalogue. "The one on the right is the subject catalogue, it will direct you to the book you need."

Five minutes later, he stood at the counter with an armload of books, and she quickly gave him a temporary borrower number, using his driver's license for identification. He smiled, noting her interest in the books he dropped on the desk.

"Is there a local newspaper?" he asked as she stamped the books, avoiding looking directly at him. She reached under the counter and handed him a thin paper, folded in half.

"It's not the New York Times, but it is full of local news. You can have my copy, I've finished with it." She blushed as his fingers brushed hers as he reached for the paper and the books. She certainly was a timid little thing. She could do with a few days away from this little hick town.

"Thank you, for the paper and the books. I'll probably be back in a couple of days to use the computer again." He smiled down at her and her blush deepened.

"If there is anything else you need to find your way around town, just give me a call." She wrote her number on the back of his temporary library card and handed it to him.

Josh looked up at her curiously, wondering if she was hitting on him or if it was a genuine offer of help. He leaned towards the latter. He had a legendary reputation with women, but the reaction from Miss Lizzy Sweet was different to the usual adoring attention of his fans.

God, she'd never even heard of him, something he really was not used to. This really was Hicksville, he just hoped the three months went by quickly. Maybe he'd ask her out, might be a nice way to pass the time.

She cleared her throat nervously. "Um...I have to lock up now, we only have a couple of minutes to get out."

He realised he was still staring, and she looked extremely nervous. He thanked her again, put her card in his pocket and headed for his Porsche as the front door of the library locked behind him.

Chapter 3

Lizzy sniffed the air as she ran lightly down the back steps of the library building to her car. A storm was brewing and she could feel the buildup of ozone in the air. Deep purple clouds swirled across the summer sky and the sighing of the tree branches soothed her uneasiness. For the first time in her life, and that was a very long time, she was unsettled by a mortal.

A mortal man.

She had been attracted to men over the centuries and had her share of sexual escapades, but never with a mortal. She could not understand where this sudden attraction came from. It was not as though he was particularly handsome, in fact, he was quite ordinary in the looks department. Despite that, she couldn't take her eyes off him. It was out of character, it had made her even more nervous and clumsy than usual, which unfortunately was fairly often.

Josh was tall, with slumberous brown eyes and a strong jaw, she noticed the cute little dimple in the centre of his chin when he had arrived clean-shaven this afternoon. Shaggy long hair of a nondescript brown, but then, she had always liked long hair. She closed her eyes. His body was nice, not made for bodybuilding, but one that she would put in the warm and cuddly category.

She was going to have to cast a serious spell tonight to remove this mortal from her thoughts. The storm building in the east provided the perfect background for spell casting. The lightning played around the edges of the purple clouds as the sky darkened. A clap of thunder rumbled in the distance and Lizzy lifted her face to the elements, smiling to herself as she remembered those warm brown eyes. Closing her eyes, she visualised his arms around her. A warm contentment snuck over her and she smiled as she drifted off into dreams of Josh. Maybe the spell could wait a day or so...

On the way home, she turned her car into Mrs. Macpherson's driveway, pleased to see the big black motorbike parked on the kerb. As usual, Wesley had left his chores until the end of the day and Lizzy smiled as the roar of the lawn mower came around from the back garden in the dusk light. Lightly tapping on the door, she sighed appreciatively as the smell of baking bread drifted across her nostrils. The thumping of the old lady's walking cane on the bare floorboards preceded the rattling of the chain on the door.

"Oh, Lizzy, come away in from the heat."

"Only a quick visit, Mrs. Mac, I want to get home before the storm breaks. I just called in to return your lunch box. Did Wesley tell you we enjoyed the sandwiches?" Mrs. Macpherson smiled and put her hand on Lizzy's arm.

"Making your lunch is the least I can do, to thank you for the way you care for me, girl."

Lizzy had spent a great deal of time over the last fifty years, looking after the elderly folk of the valley. She weeded gardens, made them herbal potions and generally kept

32

an eye on their well-being. She had taken over the role from her grandmother, moving into the little cottage when Gran moved to the Florida Keys to the warmer weather.

"My old bones need some warmth, Lizzy," said Gran.

Lizzy burst out laughing as her svelte blonde grandmother talked about her old bones. She kept in touch with the women of her family. Her mother and sisters were scattered across the world, comfortably settled with warlocks of their choice, living normal lives. Or as normal a life as witches and warlocks could live in a mortal world. Lizzy was the exception, never feeling the need to settle down with one man. The curse of the old crone had meant a solitary life, but she was happy and content. Or had been content, until Joshua Deegan pushed his way through the library door this morning. Mrs. Macpherson interrupted her musing.

"Take this bread home and give some to Wesley too. Leave it on the porch for him, dear. I enjoy watching him in the garden, especially with his shirt off." The little old lady giggled like a young girl. "He is built."

"Mrs. Mac, you are naughty," laughed Lizzy. "I'll give him the bread on my way out."

"I don't know why you don't settle down with that boy. He really loves you, you know. "Mrs. Macpherson sounded sad.

"No, he doesn't. He is in love with himself." Lizzy reached over and gave the frail little lady a hug. "Now, come on up and I'll help you get settled for the night. "

Mrs. Macpherson leaned on her as they climbed the stairs to the bedroom and Lizzy made sure that all of her medicines and the telephone were in easy reach. She was ninety years old and nearing the end of her time.

"Lizzy, I put a parcel on the table downstairs for you. I thought you might be interested." The old lady looked at her from under lowered lids. "One of my grandchildren sent me some of Helen's grandson's music. He is going to move to her farm."

"Oh…he's already arrived," said Lizzy slowly. "There was a cowboy in the library today borrowing some books on ghosts."

Mrs. Macpherson laughed until she wheezed, tears streaming down her face. Lizzy searched through the pills on the night table, until she found the puffer.

"Oh, what fun, Helen always said she wasn't going to move on until she had her nephew settled. Apparently, he is some hot shot in the music business and she left him the farmhouse so he would come down here and smell the roses."

Lizzy was thoughtful, as she let herself out of the old lady's house, warm bread in one hand and *"The Best of Josh Deegan"* in the other. He had already started with the roses, it would be interesting to hear what he had to sing about and how he handled the supernatural in the valley. She would have to speak to Aunt Helen.

Leaving a cob of warm bread in a snowy cloth on the front porch table, she dropped her bread and the CD in her car before strolling around the back of the cottage to see Wesley. He had finished mowing the grass and he stood in the dusk light occasionally silhouetted by the flashes of lighting.

Lizzy caught her breath at the sheer beauty of him as he watered the herb garden, clad in a pair of cut off denim jeans and nothing else. Her gaze lingered on his broad golden shoulders, glistening with perspiration. The bluish lights in his long black hair reflected the lightning and his white teeth flashed as he turned to greet her. A sneaky grin crossed his face and she backed away as he turned the hose toward her.

"Don't even think about it, Wesley."

"Lizzy, dear, you look so hot." She squealed and ran as the cool water from the hose arced in the soft light, dousing her head in a stream of cool water. As she stood dripping wet, her hair plastered to her face, she shook her fist at him. "You are an immature child, Wesley Gordon."

Turning the hose off at the tap, he strolled over and threaded her wet hair through his fingers, squeezing the water from it, and she shivered as it ran down her neck. The smile that started to curve her lips died away, he'd moved in closer and the hands moved from her hair down to her shoulders. In a defensive gesture, her hand slammed against his chest, pushing him back.

"I came here to help Mrs. Macpherson, not to play childish games with you, Wesley." He dipped his head, kissing her lightly on the lips. Scowling at him, she ran back to the car, shaking the water from her hair.

"There's some bread on the porch for you." She waved goodbye to Mrs. Macpherson, smiling down affectionately at them from her window.

Chapter 4

Josh crouched in front of the old stove and set a flame to the kindling he had chipped in the barn. Fat raindrops had sent him scurrying inside for cover, his arms protecting the firewood he had gathered from the old woodshed. A rueful grin crossed his face as he settled into the old rocking chair trying to catch the slight breeze blowing in the front door, a long way from the air con in his Nashville apartment. He rifled the pantry for a meal, and a tin of chicken soup warmed on the stove after he finally got the fire going. The heat of the fire under the stove added to the hot summer evening and he sighed. Not even a microwave oven in the kitchen. This house was doing his head in. His mysterious night visitor was trying to frighten him out of the farmhouse. He couldn't talk to anyone, his iPad had no connection, his mobile phone had no service and he was missing thousands of tweets and face book updates. How the hell was he going to stay on top of his business?

The trip from Nashville had taken two days, and when he arrived close to midnight on Friday night he had crawled into his old bed without even unpacking the Porsche. He dropped into an exhausted sleep, waking when an almighty crash reverberated through the house. Glancing at the illuminated dial of his Rolex, he sighed when he saw it was only two o'clock. Another loud crash came from downstairs and he swung his legs from the bed and listened intently. Regular clangs and crashes came up the stairway, it sounded like an animal had got into the kitchen. Creeping down the old staircase in his boxers, bare feet silent on the wooden floor, a squeaky step screeched in the darkness frightening the life out of him. It also put an end to the clanging in the kitchen.

He crept around the corner, holding his breath and hit the light switch. The kitchen was empty. Pots and pans were all over the kitchen cabinets and the old combustion stove was alight. Josh shook his head in confusion and crossed to the back door, rattling the lock. It was secure. He crept silently to the living room, the hairs standing on the back of his neck as he stood in the doorway of the dark room, listening for any movement. Nothing. Checking the rest of the house, he saw no one or any sign of a break in. Whoever had broken in was long gone, and they had locked the door behind them. He returned to bed, grumpy and unsettled, but fell asleep immediately sleeping uninterrupted until bright sunlight slanted across his eyes. The smell of baking bread and coffee teased his nostrils and his stomach rumbled in anticipation as he slowly woke.

His eyes flew open and he sat bolt upright in bed. He was alone in the house, and there were no neighbors for miles. Sniffing the air, he could almost taste the coffee. Pulling on his jeans, he walked quietly downstairs, determined to surprise the kitchen visitor. He crept across to the kitchen door and slowly pushed it open. The room was empty and silent, the aromas gone, no sign of coffee or food. The pots and pans were all neatly stacked in the cupboard, and the stove was cold. Scratching his head, he must have been more tired last night than he thought. What a strange dream.

The following night, just after midnight, another almighty crash woke Josh. Again, he crept around the house in the dark, but there was no sign of an intruder, either human or animal. In the hours before dawn, he inhaled aromas of minestrone, fresh bread, his favorite citrus tart, and pot roast.

On Sunday night, decidedly cranky from lack of sleep, lack of connectivity and the lack of progress on the songwriting front, Josh crept outside the kitchen door. He sat in the dark, a large piece of firewood by his side as he waited for his mysterious visitor to appear. No one was going to chase him away from his inheritance.

As he waited, snatches of a song flitted through his head and he hummed the melody under his breath, trying to hold it in his thoughts. At two o'clock precisely, the kitchen light came on. His head jerked around, his blood running cold as he saw the top of Aunt

Helen's bouffant hairstyle through the window. Rubbing his hand over his eyes, he turned and looked again. Sure enough, the beehive bun was bobbing along the gap above the lace curtains.

Josh closed his gaping mouth as the cold air hit his throat and he fought back a cough. Creeping along the porch, he stood outside the kitchen window, his body rigid with shock. Pots bubbled merrily on the stove and the warm aroma of baking bread hit his nostrils once more. Crackling flames reached merrily for the chimney in the fireplace, and steam rose from the hot, soapy water, where pots and pans soaked in the old stone sink.

Swallowing nervously, he reached for the doorknob, and tapped lightly on the kitchen door.

"Come in, son." Aunt Helen's cheery voice welcomed him.

Closing his eyes in disbelief, he pushed open the door and entered the kitchen.

A cold, empty kitchen. A couple of empty pans sitting on the stove, the fireplace cold and dark.

He sat for a long time on the porch, waiting for the night to die. As fingers of dawn mist settled on the fields surrounding the house, he pushed himself wearily to his feet and went back to bed.

Flicking through the library books, as he waited for his soup to heat, it soon became clear they were a waste of time. He laughed as he read some of the passages on removing ghosts.

"Ensure that the energies in and around your home are positive and that the occupants and visitors are not attracting ghosts of a negative nature."

Not a ghost of a negative nature, it's her house. I'm the intruder. The clattering of pots and pans sounds the same as it did when I was a boy. Aunt Helen was a great cook, he had loved coming to visit in the summer vacation.

Begin by cleaning your house with purified water and then protect it by imagining a bright light covering your house and protecting you and the other occupants.

This will give you an invisible yet powerful shield against unwanted ghosts.

Oh, Lordy, give me a break. He grinned as his foot began to tap, and his fingers twitched as the words of a song drifted through his head. He ran for his computer, it was the first time in a year he had felt the itch. His fingers flew furiously across the keyboard as the song wrote itself.

The acrid smell of burning soup roused him some time later, and he put the computer aside, groaning as he saw the mess in the kitchen. Not only was the soup stuck black and burned on the bottom of the pan, the entire contents of the saucepan cupboard were stacked neatly on the old scrubbed table in the middle of the room. And he hadn't heard a thing.

He looked around the room. It was a lovely space, bunches of herbs still hung drying around the window, and a line of glass bottles on the windowsill, held a variety of unfamiliar ingredients. He soaked the pan in the old stone sink, and thoughtfully put the pans back in the cupboard.

Cooking some toast and opening a tin of jelly, he carried his meal to the chair in the parlour, picking up the newspaper and browsed the local news. Turning the page, a small advertisement discretely tucked at the bottom of the public notices caught his eye. He sat up straight, reading the small text with interest.

Ghost hunter, available in the Silverton Valley. Telephone 6127265. Carefully tearing the information from the newspaper, he placed it in his pocket, determined to give it some serious consideration. After all he had a whole summer stretching ahead of him.

***

The first frog set up a croaking as the storm passed over to the next valley, and a woman of dazzling beauty perched on a low branch of a tall birch tree at the back of Lizzy's cottage garden. She smiled as her son materialised next to her.

"Be careful, my lad, stay behind this young woman so she does not see us."

Cupid frowned. "But we are rendered invisible from mortal eye sight are we not, Mother?

A soft tinkling laugh from Venus, "My son, she is not mortal. That is why the wager is unattainable."

Cupid glared at his mother, why was he destined to be easily duped?

"She is a witch." Venus settled more comfortably against the narrow branch. "Watch, she fights it with her spells, but 'twill do her no good. Your arrow is imbued with power. It is an arrow of mystical energy not magic, so her spell will not work. But she is a witch with strong will power. She will fight this love. It will be fun to watch."

"Well," replied Cupid. "I shall send an arrow to the one she admires and she will have to fight twice as hard." He could see the success of his wager disappearing.

Slowly, silently the full moon walked the night as Lizzy sat cross-legged in a circle of red candles on the damp grass in her back garden. Tall trumpet lilies bowed their heads elegantly to the moonlight, silver licorice

46

plants formed long draping sweeps illuminated by the soft light. The vanilla scent of white heliotrope mingled with the sweet smoke drifting across her hands, as they rested lightly in her lap. Voices whispered in the silver birch trees and she chanted softly under her breath, repeating the incantation twenty one times.

Unwanted love leave me be, cease your ardor, my warm regards have no path.

At the end of each seventh incantation, Lizzy lit another candle and closed her eyes to begin the next round. When she finished and the candles died, she stood, stretching, her body and soul renewed, clear of any carnal desires. She frowned. It had been a most peculiar day. Her body yearned for Josh, and now for the first time in thirty years, Wesley's naked chest stayed in her mind.

Chapter 5

Josh drove into town the next morning, looking for a public telephone. Sleeping on it, he had decided to call the ghost hunter, after all there was nothing to lose apart from his reputation as a sane person. All he needed was some advice. It seemed Aunt Helen was still around trying to tell him something and he would find out how he could help the dear old soul pass on, or through, or wherever it was that spirits went. The trip to the library had unearthed nothing apart from an acquaintance with a very attractive local, despite her dreadful homespun garb. He patted his pocket, checking he had the two numbers he needed. Definitely a way to pass some time, over the next three months.

Parking his Porsche across from the library, he strode into the county office and waited at the information counter to find out if there was a public telephone in this town,

48

and more embarrassingly, to find out what he needed to use one.

Ten minutes later, he entered the general store, coins jingling in his pocket and sat down at a red telephone. Retrieving the two numbers from his pocket, he laid them side by side on the counter, his eyes narrowing as he read off the two numbers and realised they were identical.

This town was getting more interesting by the day. Timid little Miss Sweet, was not only the local librarian, but was also the ghost hunter or shared a telephone number with the ghost hunter. Dropping the coins in the slot, he listened as the phone clicked over to a message at the other end.

"Hello, you've reached Lizzy Sweet. Please leave a message and your number and I will return your call as soon as I can."

Josh hung up without leaving a message and headed for the library. Pushing open the door, he stepped back to let a couple dressed in white exit. Whistling to himself quietly, he checked out the long tanned legs of the woman walking down the steps. As he

49

ogled at her legs disappearing up into a brief
white skirt, he bumped into a tall man with
long black hair tied back in a ponytail. Dark
hostile eyes looked him up and down, and the
taller man blocked his entry before grunting at
him rudely and pushing past him. Josh
shrugged and joined the queue at the counter,
watching Lizzy process the books for a
continuous stream of old people. She was
wearing a brown cardigan that clashed with
the silver of her hair. Dangling silver earrings,
swung jauntily from her ears. He looked at her
with male appreciation, she had such a
delicate little face. A lot of eye candy in the
library today. Maybe it wasn't Hicksville after
all.

He waited patiently, swatting absently
at a mosquito buzzing around his head,
grimacing as it found the soft skin on the side
of his neck. Reaching the counter, he pulled
the advertisement from his pocket and looked
up into beautiful grey eyes. His head spun and
his vision blurred for a moment. With shaking
hands, he clutched at his stomach as the room
tilted. He struggled for words and his

stumbling voice sounded to him as though it came from afar.

"Er...ah... er...good morning." He knew a silly grin was plastered across his face, and he couldn't do a damn thing about it. He looked at her sweet face, her beautiful eyes full of humour and warmth, returning his gaze as though she was also mesmerised.

"G...g...good morning, Mr. Deegan. Would you like to book the...er...computer again?"

"Ah...not at the moment. I was hoping you would spend your life...I mean...have lunch with me?"

She stood up slowly behind the desk and reached both hands out to him. As she shook her head, his heart broke into a thousand pieces. Taking her hands, he looked down at them, marveling at their softness and beauty. His gaze travelled up her arms and elegant neck and locked with her beautiful silver eyes.

"I can't," she apologised, looking as though her heart was breaking as well. "I have lunch with my friend."

"I need your services… that is… if this is you?" He dropped one hand to the advertisement. "I think I might need a ghost hunter. That is, I don't believe in ghosts, but I need to talk to someone who does, and I thought a ghost hunter would." He babbled in desperation, as his heart seemed to swell in his chest, and he caught his breath.

"Will you have lunch with me? Please?" He closed his eyes, trying to regain his equilibrium. Who was this bumbling fool who had taken over his brain and mouth?

Opening his eyes, he held his breath as she glanced up at the clock near the door. His heartbeat slowed, beating in time with the second hand as it moved slowly around, until she finally nodded. He started breathing again, filled with an intense joy. It pervaded his entire body, he had never felt this good. It was an even bigger rush than standing on stage in front of fifty thousand screaming fans.

"As long as you don't mind sharing lunch with my friend as well? Can you meet me at the picnic table in the park across the square in fifteen minutes?"

He smiled and nodded without speaking. Josh Deegan was in love for the first time in his life.

**

Lizzy spent ten minutes preparing for lunch in front of the mirror in the rest room. Reapplying her lipstick with shaking hands, she ran her fingers through the silvery strands of hair, lifting it away from her perspiring neck. Nerves and the continuing summer heat in a building without air conditioning left her flushed and perspiring. As she leaned closer to the mirror, she spotted the mosquito bite on the side of her neck. Eyes narrowing, she examined the heart shaped bite. Scrabbling through the depths of her handbag, she retrieved her mirror and held the magnifying side to her neck.

Her heart skipped a beat as she saw the perfect small pink heart on her skin. No wonder her spell of last night had dissipated as soon as Josh Deegan stood in front of her counter. She was dealing with physical energy here, not magic. She recalled a story of Cupid and his magic arrows, at her grandmother's knee but had paid no heed to the legend since that time.

She thought back to yesterday, remembering the strange little man in the white suit following her, when she felt the sting on her neck. Why had Cupid chosen her, a witch, as his target? Surely the gods were smart enough to know that an immortal was able to dispel the lust of such an arrow?

Josh must think she was a clumsy fool, although on second thoughts, he had been acting pretty strangely himself. Taking one last look at her appearance, she locked the library, picking up the lunch box on the way out. Walking thoughtfully across the park, Lizzy looked up at the two men sitting across from each other at the picnic table. She smothered a grin as the antagonism sizzled in the air between them. Wesley's aura was red with suppressed anger and a dark pink aura surrounded Josh. Sliding onto the bench next to Wesley, she placed her hand on his arm sending him a silent message to calm down before she spoke.

"Wes, we have some business to discuss with Mr. Deegan. Have you introduced yourself?"

Wesley scowled at her. "Yes, we've met. Mr. Deegan has been most interested in you. He has been asking lots of questions." Wesley looked very unhappy.

"None of which Mr. Gordon would answer," growled Josh. He looked over at Lizzy and smiled sweetly. Resting his elbow on the table, he dropped his chin in his hand and stared at her without blinking.

Lizzy took a deep breath and reached for the courage to look back at Josh, as she pulled the lunch box from her bag. Eyes narrowing, her gaze followed his fingers absently scratching at his neck.

"Josh... turn your head to the side." Lizzy narrowed her eyes, her voice anxious.

Wesley turned his head swiftly at the distress in her voice and he jumped to his feet, reaching across the table and grabbing Josh by the shirtfront.

"Stop leering at her, you pervert. I've a good mind to turn you into a frog." He put his face up close to Josh and eyeballed him.

"Wesley Gordon, sit back down." Lizzy reached across the table and pulled his hands away from Josh. "Now."

"What exactly have I got myself into in this hick town?" Josh looked up at them both, confusion written all over his face.

"Ghosts, crazy overgrown boys, frogs?" He stood and glared at Wesley, throwing an apologetic glance Lizzy's way. He bunched his fists in front of his chest.

"Do your best, boyo."

Wesley stood, fists bunched, and Lizzy grabbed his hands again before he could lunge across the table. She placed a turkey and brie sandwich in front of each of them before she spoke, her voice cold.

"Unless the two of you can behave like civil human beings"— glaring at Wesley as he snickered—"I will have my lunch elsewhere and the two of you can take a flying leap into the mill pond."

The two men sat down reluctantly, continuing to glare across the table at each other.

"Now Josh, tell me exactly why you need a ghost hunter." As she turned to look at Josh, his hand reached out, brushing the back of her knuckles and warmth invaded her body. From the corner of her eye, she saw Wesley roll his eyes, as she helplessly locked her gaze with Josh.

Chapter 6

Another storm was building as Lizzy turned her little old car onto the track leading to Aunt Helen's farmhouse. No, she corrected herself, it was Josh Deegan's farmhouse now, or it soon would be. Tapping lightly on the kitchen door, she sniffed appreciatively at the wood smoke drifting from the chimney. The door opened and those beautiful brown eyes crinkled in a smile as he ushered her through the doorway into the welcoming kitchen. She had always loved this room and had spent many of Helen's last months, preparing herbals to relieve her pain.

"It's lovely to see the stove alight," she said stupidly, looking away from him. She felt him step toward her as a log popped in the fire and the embers drifted lazily up the stove chimney. Even though she knew why she felt so helpless, her will was gone, and she could not move as his hands gently cradled her face. Her limbs were weightless and her heart

58

thudded. A strange mist fell before her eyes and she blinked. Finding the courage to look at him, a soft moan escaped her lips. The mist lifted as a future with this mortal flashed before her eyes. Their gazes held, and she sank into the warm brown depths of his eyes as his lips moved toward her neck. Her mouth dropped open, her breath coming in short soft pants. This was what she wanted, this mindless mating of the flesh. Nothing else mattered to her in that moment.

Nerve endings sizzled as the warmth of his mouth moved from the little pink heart on her neck, along her jaw, sliding to a stop at the side of her lips. The roughness of unshaven skin against her soft cheek left her face tingling. He paused. Gently pushing her away, he looked deep into her eyes, wordlessly seeking permission to kiss her. She closed the space between them and offered her lips to him.

HIs gentle lips closed on her mouth, warmth suffused her entire body and her stomach tightened. She arched against Josh craving completion.

59

But his mouth stayed gentle, his tongue seeking permission to dance. Lizzy opened her lips in acceptance, almost sobbing as his breath mingled with hers. His hands cradled her face with reverence, her hands reached around and locked behind his neck, pulling his head down to her. She was sure she would stop breathing if his mouth broke from hers.

As her fingers brushed the pink raised heart on his neck, a chill engulfed her and her heart stilled. The coldness pervaded her limbs, and she grabbed his hands away from her face pushing them away.

"No." Her voice rose as his hands moved back to her shoulders. "No. Stop. I said no."

Backing away, she stared at him, wide eyed and hands clenched behind her back. She stepped back until she reached the counter on the other side of the kitchen. Josh's eyes widened in distress and he held a hand out to her in apology.

"Lizzy, I am so sorry." His face was aghast with horror. "I don't know what came over me."

He stepped toward her and she shrank back against the counter, feeling the blood drain from her face.

"Don't touch me." She was terrified.

He stopped, both hands raised in front of his chest, trying to soothe her from across the kitchen.

"It's alright, calm down, I won't hurt you." He moved one step closer.

"Don't come near me," her voice sounded shrill even above the drumming in her ears. "It will kill me."

A stray lock of hair fell across his forehead, and Josh ran an impatient hand through his shaggy hair, in a move that was becoming achingly familiar to her.

"Lizzy, I am not going to hurt you. I'm not a monster. I genuinely asked you here to help me sort out my problem with this house." He looked at her with pleading eyes and she almost ran across the room into his arms.

"Please trust me," he begged.

"I trust you, Josh. It's me. I'm the problem." She breathed deeply willing herself

61

to regain her composure. A measure of calm stole over her as her breathing leveled.

She smiled ruefully, turning her head and touching the pink heart on her neck.

"This is what came over us, Josh." His brow furrowed in confusion as his gaze followed her fingers to the small pink heart on her neck.

"A birthmark?" he asked quizzically.

"No, not a birthmark. Feel the side of your neck," she replied.

His right hand reached up and rubbed across his neck. His fingers stilled as they encountered the small raised mark on the side of his neck.

"My mosquito bite?"

"Er…not exactly," she replied quietly. "I'll explain later. In the meantime, just keep your distance."

"Look, I'm sorry…" She interrupted him before he could finish speaking.

"No, I mean keep your distance, because we are both of the same inclination, if we get close to each other, we won't be able to keep our hands off each other." Her voice was impatient.

He turned away from her reluctantly and moved across to the old sink, filling the kettle.

"Coffee?" She ignored his question, her attention totally focused on his face.

"Do you believe in ghosts, Josh?" she asked quietly.

He laughed uneasily, shaking his head. "If you had asked me that a couple of days ago I would have said you were crazy, but honestly now I don't know."

"What about witches?" She paused. "Magic, spells and potions?"

"Give me a break," he said, running his fingers through his shaggy hair. She was silent as she gathered her thoughts.

"You've been here for a week, haven't you Josh?" she asked softly.

He nodded.

"Have you felt your Aunt Helen's presence?"

He looked at her without answering as a strong gust of wind rattled the kitchen windows. The storm clouds scurried across the moon, the sky cleared and a shaft of moonlight shone through the kitchen window. Lizzy stood bathed in moonlight, the lace of the curtains fracturing the beam, and the power of the moon goddess entered her strengthening her will.

"Thank you, mother," she breathed, her eyes closing as she let the power do its work. She stood motionless for a full minute.

"Lizzy, are you alright?" Josh sounded wary.

She stood tall and straight, holding her hand out to him. "It's alright Josh, I'm sorry I upset you."

He hesitated before crossing the kitchen and taking her hand. The look of adoration in his eyes sent sparks running along her nerve endings, all she needed was his touch. Closing her eyes, Lizzy focused on the power within, to resist succumbing to temptation once again.

"I can't tell you what is happening yet, I need to do some thinking." She squeezed his hand to reassure him. "In the meantime, I will leave you some smudge sticks to burn in the kitchen before you go to bed and I will say a little incantation to help clear the negative energy away."

"What's a smudge stick?" Josh sounded skeptical.

"Just some white sage from my garden, and I'll leave you a feather to fan it into the corners."

Josh burst out laughing, and Lizzy turned away to hide how much his laughter hurt. A single laugh reminded her why she could never be with a mortal, especially a sceptic.

"Please go outside for a moment, Josh." She asked, turning her head as she surreptitiously brushed away a tear.

He released her hand and went out to the porch. She whispered the words to begin the cleansing, knowing it would take a few more visits to help Helen across to the spirit world.

"Quick or dead, I will feed you,
Cease to grieve and take your leave"

Helen, I bid you depart, but should you remain

Be calm, take heart I will return again.

Lizzy drove home, gulping back sobs as the tears streamed down her face. As she neared her cottage, she made a sudden decision and turned back to town.

***

Josh wandered around the kitchen with a taper from the fire, feeling like an idiot as he lit a smudge stick in each corner. He ignored the feather Lizzy had left on the counter. As the sharp aroma of burning sage wafted through the kitchen, he moved into the living room, picked up his guitar and sat in front of the fire. He caught himself staring into space, the guitar sitting on his lap and a stupid grin on his face. Shaking his head, he took a deep breath. Why was he fixated on the little librarian in this hick town? Absolutely not his style. He could forget about her when she was not around, but it was like he lost control of his emotions whenever she came near him. Was this love? His fingers plucked at the guitar strings and the melody poured from the instrument, as the words came from his heart. He sang the song twice, before putting his guitar aside and reaching for his computer.

***

Lizzy turned into the main street of Silverton, and did not see a single soul. The town went to bed as soon as it was dark, mostly old folk remained in the valley and there were very few young people in the town. Pulling quietly into Wesley's driveway, she took a deep breath, hoping her plan would work. At least Wesley should be happy with her decision tonight.

Walking along the path, flowers nodding in welcome, she inhaled the spicy aromas of his garden. The moon was full and heavy, the shadowy corners of the garden filled with the rustling of small creatures. She tapped at the front door, waiting impatiently, but the loud rock music thumping through the house muffled her knocking. She rattled the doorknob, and rang the bell to no avail.

"The one time I really need you, Wesley." She muttered nervously to herself as she walked around to the back garden, sighing with relief as she saw the soft light shining through the back windows.

Stepping onto Wesley's back porch, she stopped, taking a deep breath as the flickering candlelight blurred the scene before her. Wesley stretched out on his day bed, surrounded by plump silk cushions in a myriad of brilliant colours. Hundreds of red rose petals surrounded him, on the bed and on the floor. Dozens of white candles lit the small room and two wine goblets sat at his elbow on a silver tray, an uncorked bottle of golden liquid waiting.

"I've been waiting for you, Lizzy." He almost purred, his voice was deep and sexy

Sparks flew from her fingertips as she pointed at him, her temper instantly at flashpoint.

"You knew I would come. You slimy, selfish little toad," Lizzy hissed the worst insult she could lay her tongue to. "You cheating, despicable, worm-ridden piece of shit."

Wesley lay back on the bed, casting a baleful glance in her direction as he uncorked the bottle. As the wine slid sensuously down the side of the goblet, he turned to her. His voice was sad and his beautiful deep blue eyes were as cold as ice.

"For years, I have waited for you to come to me, and tonight you come, so I can scratch the itch you will not allow the mortal to ease."

"You looked. I can't believe you looked." Lizzy screeched at him like a banshee even as the tears wet her cheeks. "You promised me, Wes."

Stretching lazily, Wesley eased himself off the soft bed, his white robe floating around his legs as he walked toward her.

"Yes, I looked because I worried for you. Even though you know what causes this lust you feel for the mortal, I worried you would succumb." His voice broke. "If you do, I will lose you…forever." He paused and the flames of the candles danced in his dark eyes. Walking over to the doorway, he turned and the look on his face almost broke her heart.

"Forever, Lizzy. I would not survive. So yes, I looked."

Her temper died and as she looked at Wesley, a strange tightness banded her chest. She reached out for him but he turned away from her.

"What did you see?" She stumbled over the words.

"Go home. I know you're safe." His beautiful blue eyes glowed as he turned back to her. "For now."

The tears slid silently down her cheeks for the second time that night, as Lizzy drove slowly home.

Chapter 7

If Aunt Helen visited or baked that night, Josh remained oblivious to any action. For the first time in many months, the creative urge consumed him, his fingers flying over the keyboard as he typed lyrics and coded notes into the music program on his computer.

"Six songs, Reuben," Josh held the red phone close to one ear, his hand over the other to block the loud conversation at the counter in the dusty old general store.

"Yes, buddy, I said six songs and they're all good stuff." Josh was almost jumping out of his skin. "Different to usual," he explained to his agent. "A little bit more fey." He laughed at the response from the other end. "I don't know, a little bit of magic, a few ghosts and a pretty lady...yes, Reuben, even here in Hicksville."

He put the phone down a few minutes later, promising to deliver another four songs and be ready to lay down a new album as soon as he came home. The store was quiet and he looked up to a circle of disapproving faces. An old man leaning on a walking stick, wagged a finger at him.

"You need to watch your mouth, young man. Your Aunt Helen was an upstanding member of this community and if you are not careful, I will tell our Lizzy you think you have landed in Hicksville."

The elderly lady serving behind the counter scowled at him.

"Besides, young man, that pretty lady is already spoken for. Why, she is almost engaged to that lovely young man who mows our lawns and tends our gardens."

"Wesley Gordon, they have been walking out for twenty years or more," interjected another old man.

Josh's head flew up and he narrowed his eyes. "Twenty years?"

Another old lady leaned on her stick and glared back at him. "Probably closer to thirty."

Josh stood and nodded his thanks to the storekeeper as he pushed his way out the door, past sacks of flour and shovels and assorted farm implements. Thirty years. He sure had landed on the funny farm. Frowning, he crossed the road to the library.

Pushing open the door, he was pleased to see Lizzy alone behind the counter.

"Do you run this place by yourself?" he asked. Her head flew up and twin spots of red burned on her cheeks. He noted her hand shaking as she reached up to pull her hair back. She flashed him a pretty smile, before she nodded. He stared at her, his groin tightening instantly.

"Lunch, just you and me?" he asked quietly.

"Lunch, you, me and Wesley," she answered. "It's a longstanding arrangement. One of our old friends makes our lunch every day, I run some chores for her, and Wes mows her grass.

She dropped her head and waited for his reply.

"Okay, as long as he doesn't threaten me again," he laughed. "What was the frog comment yesterday? He has a smart mouth."

"Wes is very protective, he always looks out for me." Silver hair swung around her beautiful delicate face and the opening lines of his next song flitted through his head.

"Is the computer free?" he asked urgently, wanting to get the words down quickly before he lost them.

"Just happens to be," she smiled at him. "You can have it for the half hour until lunchtime."

He drifted off in his creative mind as he typed away on the old computer, three verses and a chorus about a pretty lady with magical powers, ensnaring a hapless man. Very satisfied, he emailed them to himself, updated his social networking sites with his whereabouts, and created a very funny, or at least he thought it was funny, blog about life in Hicksville. He was careful not to mention Silver Valley in his blog as he didn't want any more trouble from the locals. Although, he doubted they had ever heard of the internet, let alone used it.

He felt a light tap on his shoulder. Looking up at Lizzy, his world shifted, as instant hunger rushed through his veins.

"I'll meet you over at the park, I'm about to lock up." She paused as he stood. "And please be nice to Wesley."

***

Josh sat alone at the table and Lizzy groaned as she walked toward him. Her eyes scanned the park and the roadway for Wesley or his motorbike. Only a couple of old farm trucks drove sedately down the street and there was no sign of Wesley. Placing her hand on Josh's arm, she looked him up and down for any sign of injury or bewitching.

"Was he terribly rude to you?"

Josh shrugged. "Wesley? Haven't seen him. The park was empty."

Lizzy hid her distress as she pulled out the lunch box. She handed a sandwich to Josh, already missing Wesley and his smart comments, sneaky kisses and wandering hands. Josh folded the greaseproof paper into

75

a small square and placed it neatly under the lunchbox. Lizzy automatically reached for her coffee, and then realised there was none today without Wesley.

No Wesley. She frowned. No joy in the day.

She wanted to talk to him and sort things out, although she worried that was a long way off. Maybe she owed him an apology. Okay, maybe she owed him a big apology, she truly had made a bad decision yesterday and she knew Wesley was licking his wounds somewhere. He'd been hitting on her for thirty years and the one time she offered herself to him, he had taken offence. She shook her head angrily, she knew she was being unfair to him.

"Penny for them?" She looked up into Josh's warm brown eyes and a shaft of longing shivered straight up her legs. She blushed, dropping her head as the warmth stopped between her thighs.

"Tell me a bit about yourself, Lizzy. How long have you lived in the valley?" His tone was curious. Obviously one of the old folk had been talking to him.

"Quite a while," she replied warily." I moved into my grandmother's cottage when she retired to Florida." She didn't tell him it was back in 1947, but quickly changed the subject.

"Tell me about you? Where do you come from, Josh?"

"I grew up in Chicago, but I spent a lot of holidays in the valley as a boy," he replied. "I think I can remember your grandmother, you look just like her, although she would have been too young, maybe it was your mother I remember?"

Lizzy hid a smile, she had a vague memory of Josh tearing around as a ten year old with the local boys. They had fished in the stream at the back of her little cottage and brought her fish in exchange for the fat worms in her garden. Better he didn't know it was actually her. Wesley was the only person in her life, apart from family who knew her real age. She smiled, if she was honest with

Josh, he would jump into his flash Porsche and head non-stop for Nashville, Tennessee.

"Then I dropped out of college and moved to Nashville and started writing songs," he continued. Reaching across the table, he held her hand, turning it over and absently tracing the lines on her palm. The tingling followed his fingertips, continued up her arm and she felt a quickening in her loins and a desperate desire to tear his shirt off.

"Two hit albums and I was pretty comfortable by my mid-twenties. I have a great apartment and a great car." He nodded over at the yellow Porsche parked across from the table. "And now a farm I can sell to expand my recording studio."

She smiled. "Be careful where you park that flash car in this town. Most of the old folk park by feel."

"Why do you live here, Lizzy? It is such a hick town." She burred at that, pulling her hand out of his gentle grip.

"It's a beautiful town filled with lovely old souls. I am very happy living here."

"But what do you do?" he asked.

78

ANNIE SEATON

"Do?" Her voice was frosty.

"For fun? Entertainment? Where do you go to eat out?"

"We are very different people, Josh," she said regretfully. "I don't have those needs. Wesley and I make our own entertainment. We have picnics, we hike. Why, last summer, we hiked over fifty mikes on the Appalachian Trail and we even saw bears. We camped out for a whole week."

"Mmm...Wesley?" he said slowly. "So he is your boyfriend?"

She laughed, "No, but he is my very best friend."

"Is he gay?"

"God, no," she spluttered. She thought of the number of times she had rescued Wesley from relationships where he had wanted out, and was too polite to finish it himself. She had even cast a spell or two for him over the years.

Thoughtful, she realised she hadn't done that for a long time. In fact, she hadn't rescued him from the attentions of an irate husband for many years. Not since he had started this ridiculous story of being in love with her. She shook her head in confusion.

Josh squeezed her hand.

"Lizzy, can I take you out for dinner tomorrow night? If I can find somewhere decent to eat within a reasonable distance?"

She looked up into the allure of his soulful brown eyes.

"I'm not sure that it is wise, Josh. Maybe we had better keep a professional relationship... you know, ghost hunter and haunted house owner." She smiled at him to soften the knockback.

Josh stood and leaned across the table, taking Lizzy's face in his gentle hands.

"Please give it some thought? We can discuss some ghost hunting strategies over dinner."

"I'll let you know," she replied, pulling away from his gentle grip, the urge to kiss him was overwhelming her.

"And now I really have to get back to work." Her voice was reluctant, at odds with her words.

He reached across, dragging her into his arms. His lips descended on hers, his fingers threading through the streaming cascade of her silver hair. Lizzy returned his kiss for a long breathless interval before pulling back, and looked at him wordlessly as a caressing finger stroked her cheek.

"I'll call you," he said softly.

The afternoon dragged, and it seemed like forever until Lizzy closed the library and drove around to Wesley's house. He lived in a rambling old house on the corner of Main Street across from the millpond. Even though Wesley was quite wealthy, he had never disclosed to Lizzy the source of his significant income. He was generous, yet lived a very simple lifestyle. All his energies, human and supernatural, went into his beautiful garden. She unlatched the front gate and looked down in distress at the dead flower heads on the path under her feet. No flowers nodded in the breeze, the bees were quiet, and the usual birdsong was absent. The garden was dry and the perfume of the flowers, sharp and decayed. All the windows were closed, and their shutters down and Lizzy's stomach dropped as the deserted house looked grimly down at her.

Her neck prickling, she walked silently to the back garden, dread in every footstep. The back porch was clear of any furniture and the back door was firmly locked. Running to the garage, she rattled the side door, it was also locked and bolted.

Her stomach turned. "Oh, Mother goddess, what has he done?"

Running back to the front of the house, her breath hitching, she pounded on the front door.

"Wesley Gordon, you open this door, right this instant."

She banged on the door and yelled like a harridan, until a quavering voice by her shoulder frightened her. Turning swiftly, she almost knocked old Mr. Henry off his walker. Putting her hand on his arm, she apologised to Wesley's elderly neighbor as she steadied him.

"What's all the racket about, girl?" His voice was irritable.

"I was trying to raise Wesley," she replied breathlessly.

"Well, he's gone. Packed up and left first thing this morning. Didn't even say goodbye, the inconsiderate young rascal."

"Packed up?" Lizzy's voice was shrill. "On his motorbike?"

"No, a truck came and took a few boxes, and odds and ends, he loaded his bike in the truck and off they went."

"They? Who? Where to?"

"I don't know girl, didn't he tell you? We half thought you were finally going to let him move in with you. Mrs. Henry and I were hoping…"

Lizzy was embarrassed. "Oh, well, I am sure he will ring me tonight."

Bidding the old man farewell, she walked slowly to her car, her throat aching with the tears she held back. She knew Wesley so well. He had hidden his hurt from her. She knew she had disappointed him, she should have stayed and made her peace last night. Her heart aching, she rubbed her hands over her lips, where the taste of Josh lingered.

Damn you, Cupid. I am going to sort this out once and for all. My life was going along quite nicely, without your arrow.

On the way home, she drove into Helen's farm, a plan fixed firmly in her mind. She was not going to go within two yards of Josh, although she did yearn for just a teensy glimpse of him.

For the second time that afternoon, Lizzy pounded on a door with no answer. She threaded a note through the latch inviting Josh for dinner at her cottage on Saturday night. If all went to her plan, the lustful, sensual passion embedded in her soul would be short lived and she could then put her power to work finding Wesley.

***

Josh drove home slowly, a warm rosy feeling in his chest. He was almost bursting with happiness, despite being away from his home and city for the next eleven weeks. Closing his eyes, he brought his hand to his nose, inhaling the citrus scent that lingered on his fingers from Lizzy's hair. Eleven weeks to convince her to leave this godforsaken valley and move back to Nashville with him.

New lyrics flitted through his head and he parked the Porsche in the barn and ran for the door before they whispered off into the air. He saw the pink note in the latch and punched the air as he read the invitation.

"Yes!"

Chapter 8

Friday was Lizzy's day off work. She had to find a spell to reverse the effects of Cupid's arrow. She knew the ingredients she needed for the meal, the foods and herbs that dispelled lust, but the words of the incantation and the mix of the potion eluded her. Basket over her arm, she smiled at the nodding branches of the pear tree laden with fruit, before picking two perfect pears and placing them gently in her basket. She moved across to the magnolia tree, and found one last blossom left from the spring and added it to the pears in the basket.

The fuzzy leaves of the patchouli bush in her herb garden brushed her fingers and the spicy, aromatic smell wafted across the garden as she carefully picked the white flowers. A sprig of peppermint, six radishes and her collection was finished. She spread the herbs out to dry on the counter in the sun as she made a couple of telephone calls.

"Hey, Lizzy," her mother greeted her with delight. "Everything okay?"

"A couple of little problems, Mama." Lizzy rolled her eyes at herself in the mirror in the hallway, where she sat on the yellow velvet loveseat. Her fingers plucked at the tassels on the side of the seat. "Nothing I can't handle."

"I dreamed about you and Wesley last night, Lizzy. I am hoping it was an omen." Her mother sounded hopeful. "Have you finally succumbed to our beautiful boy?"

Lizzy held back a groan.

"Why? Have you been talking to Wesley?" she asked tentatively.

"No, just a dream. Your father and I were hoping."

"No, Mama, we are just best friends. I was actually looking for a spell."

"Have you tried the internet?"

Lizzy rolled her eyes. "No, Mama, I was hoping to find Gran's old spell book."

"You'll have to ring Gran, and Lizzy, you must get with the times. It's all at your fingertips online now."

87

"Okay, Mama. Give my love to Dad." She rang off and reluctantly called her grandmother.

"Hey, Gran, how's the heat in Florida?"

The sweet tones of her grandmother's youthful voice tinkled down the phone line.

"Hello, my dearest, I was waiting for you to call before I went to golf."

Lizzy's heart skipped a beat. "Is Wesley down there with you?"

"Now, why would you think that, you haven't been fighting with our darling boy, have you?"

"No, Gran." Lizzy glared across the foyer, watching the dust mites drift through the sunshine. *Darling boy, indeed.* They chatted for a couple more minutes.

"Gran, can I ask you something?"

"Anything, my darling girl. What can I help you with?"

"I remember once years ago you told me a story about Cupid, and leaden and golden arrows and that they were different?"

Gran sighed softly. "Yes dear, I had occasion to source a spell to dispel the physical energy once upon a time. It's a very hard thing to shift."

"What was the spell?" Lizzy asked anxiously.

"Oh, it was long ago, before I even met your Gramps. You'll find it in the attic, in my little heart-shaped spell book. You know the one full of love spells and potions. You used to love it when you were a little girl."

Lizzy was keen to ring off and run up to the attic, but Gran kept her chatting for a few more minutes.

"When are you coming to visit, sweetheart?"

"Maybe in the autumn. I'm thinking of going to Nashville for a holiday soon," replied Lizzy. Ringing off, she headed straight for the attic. Pulling down the little steps hidden in the corner of the spare room, she pushed open the small door in the ceiling and climbed into the dark room.

Choking as she disturbed the dust, she pointed at the far wall and sent a small flame from her fingertips to light the row of candles sitting on the shelf in the corner. The attic was a treasure trove of dust and spiders. Spider webs hung in garlands from the ceiling and Lizzy covered her mouth as years of dust rose and floated gently around her as she searched through the piles of old books and clothes.

"Yes!" Triumphant as she saw the corner of the little old heart-shaped book poking out of the corner of the second trunk she searched.

Clutching it to her chest, she backed through the old furniture, pointing at the candles to douse the flames, before climbing back through the hole in the ceiling and down the steps. Laughing as she caught sight of her reflection in the old mirror at the end of the hallway. She looked like an old crone, her hair covered in grey dust, smudges of dirt coloured her cheeks and her clothes were filthy. Perhaps if Josh saw her now, he would run a mile and she would not need a spell.

A quick shower, change of clothes, and a long glass of iced mint tea and she settled comfortably in the hammock on her front porch as she dipped into Gran's book. On the second last page, a picture of a little cherub holding a bow sat above the words she sought and she smiled.

Closing her eyes, she held the book as she swung gently in the morning breeze. The warm sunshine and the sound of bees buzzing as they drank from her garden lulled her off into a light doze. She dreamed of Josh and lazily flicked a finger through the window toward her stereo, and the gentle rhythm of a guitar preceded his sad voice drifting out to the porch. She smiled in her sleep as he sang of hopeless love.

'And I'm always hoping one sunny day, I'm gonna stop this runnin' around

And find my one true love, but every chance that comes ,I run the other way.

Josh reached for her in the dream, her body cocooned in warmth as she held her hands out to take his. Sweetness and joy surrounded her as his soulful brown eyes smiled back at her. He leaned in to kiss her, but his eyes turned deep blue and suddenly

Wesley looked down at her, his face alight with intense joy. She opened her mouth to him and murmured.

"My love."

She woke with a start, as the music turned into a loud thumping boot scooting song, feeling disorientated. *Where the hell had that dream come from?*

She flicked a finger at the stereo and turned the music off on the way to the kitchen. Reaching for the mortar and pestle on the windowsill, she crumbled the dried herbs into the bowl. Frowning as she pounded the patchouli leaves, her temper simmered. Why was everyone so keen to get Wesley into her bed and her life? Why did she dream of Wesley? She had a good mind to take Josh on, even after Cupid's arrow was gone and go to Nashville with him just to show her family and Wesley she was in charge of her own destiny. The pungent smell of crushed herbs surrounded her as she muttered crossly to herself.

***

Wesley Gordon turned to the beautiful blonde witch, as she carefully replaced the phone in its cradle. He raised his eyebrows as he looked at Lizzy's grandmother, so like her granddaughter, but with the knowledge of many, many more years in her grey eyes.

"Well?" he asked eagerly. "Did she seem upset?"

"Mmm, not really, a bit preoccupied. She did ask if you were here, though."

He smiled, pleased Lizzy was looking for him.

"Is she coming to find me after she dispels the energy?" He would be ready for her when she arrived.

"No," was the careful reply. "She said she is going to Nashville."

Chapter 9

Josh tapped lightly on Lizzy's door, sniffing appreciatively at the aromas wafting from the kitchen. He had been in the valley for over a week, living on bread, soup and fruit from Helen's orchard. The muse held him in a tight grip and he only left the farm to go to the library and the public phone. After his gaff in the store, he didn't feel much like going back in for another visit to buy food. The old folk would probably poison it anyway.

Lizzy stood at the door, a sheer mauve gown, floating from her shoulders. His groin tightened as the citrus smell of her hair drifted over to him, and ignoring the spike of lust, Josh reached across and gave her a gentle kiss on her soft cheek.

She seemed elusive tonight, perhaps it was the candle light silhouetting her that made her seem aloof.

"Come in, Josh. You had no trouble finding my cottage?" Her voice tinkled like crystal and her eyes looked dreamy. Remembering his manners, he pulled the bunch of scarlet roses from behind his back and handed them to her.

"Beautiful flowers for a beautiful lady." He stifled a groan.

You're a songwriter, man, and that's the best you can come up with?

Lizzy buried her face in the red petals and he was surprised to see sadness flit across the delicate features. She looked troubled, her eyes were sad tonight.

"From Helen's garden?"

"Yes, they looked like they needed company."

"They are lovely, thank you."

Lizzy ushered Josh into the living room and he caught his breath. Dozens of candle shimmered in the soft evening light. Rainbow colours reflected from dozens of crystals hanging from the window frames. The scented candles floated in bowls of flowers perfuming the room with sweetness. Pale mauve amethysts and shiny black pebbles sat next to each bowl. Aunt Helen had loved candles and flowers, he remembered. Candles and flowers and porcelain bowls.

Josh picked up a small, shiny pebble and rolled it between his fingertips. For such a cold stone, it quickly warmed his fingers.

Lizzy smiled at him. "Obsidian, for strengthening the spirit, a good choice."

Crossing to the table, she held up a long slender bottle and uncorked it, a subtle floral aroma pervading the room as she poured the pale golden liquid into two long stemmed crystal glasses.

"Apple wine." She handed him a glass and he sipped tentatively. "I make my own, from the apples in your orchard." His throat warmed the smooth liquid slipped down.

"Mmm, a potent brew."

Lizzy smiled at him, and the warmth spread to his groin. "I have prepared the guest room for you, if you would like to indulge tonight."

His head flew up, anticipation rushing through his body. Stepping over to her, he leaned over gently kissing her lips, his hands held tightly behind his back. "I would be honoured to indulge you."

"Indulge in my wine and food." She shook her head gently and smiled her secret smile. "That will be enough indulgence for the present. Sit in front of the fire, Josh. I'm glad it is cool enough for a fire tonight, it makes the room cheery. I have a couple of things to finish up in the kitchen."

He looked up feeling sheepish. "Would you think me terribly rude if I used your computer to check my emails while you are in the kitchen?"

Her soft laugh sent delicious shivers down his back. She placed her hand on his arm.

"Josh, I don't have a computer."

He felt his mouth drop open and he closed it quickly as he looked at her, trying to figure out if she was serious.

"How do you keep in touch? Where do you tweet?"

She smiled gently. "Tweet? Birds tweet."

"Twitter, Facebook, email, Instagram? How do you know what's happening?"

"I look out the window. I see the sun. I listen to the birds, that's all the tweeting I need. All I need to know, I find through people I see." Josh looked at her, astonished. In this day, he could not believe someone of his generation could be so out of touch and remain blasé about it.

"I'll have to teach you. I would love you to come and visit me when I go home to Nashville."

"No need to rush into anything," she replied. "You may find you are finished with me by then." As he looked up at her, another spike of lust hit his loins and he shook his head. "Never, Lizzy, not the way I feel about you."

"Come into the kitchen and talk to me while I work. Bring your wine."

Josh settled comfortably onto a high stool at the bench in the kitchen, and watched her slender white hands sprinkle chopped peppermint leaves over a tray of cheese, garnished with pink radishes. As she bent to the oven and removed a tray, he groaned inwardly, as the filmy dress clung to the outline of her very shapely bottom.

"Now, Josh, I want you to do something for me," Lizzy said as she pushed her hair away from her face, flushed from the heat of the oven.

"I'll do anything." He laughed, then realised he meant it. He would do anything for this beautiful woman, he had never felt like this before in his life.

"As long as those delicious aromas are my dinner, I am in your hands."

She reached for a bowl and filled it with water, placed a withered magnolia flower on the counter, and lit a candle next to the bowl.

"Close your eyes, Josh." Her voice was soft. "Clear your mind of everything, except how you are feeling right now."

He looked at her thoughtfully. "Why?"

"Trust me Josh, and trust your feelings." He closed his eyes, his hands gripping the edge of the stool. The apple wine was potent and he hadn't eaten since breakfast. Wine on an empty stomach was never kind to him. Her soft voice lulled him.

"Forget about the wine, Josh. Think about your feelings." The only thing he could feel was the tightening in his groin and the lack of blood going anywhere else. He could feel himself swell as he thought of Lizzy. She fed his masculinity and his body craved her. The candle hissed and the water dripped into the bowl. A fragrance of patchouli and mint drifted past him with a soft whisper.

'Unwanted crush and lust from thee,
Who drinks this potion will no longer see,
The attraction to his loins desire.'

His eyes flew open, unable to believe what he was hearing. He watched. Lizzy's eyes were closed as she took a petal from the dead magnolia and placed it in the bowl. She reached for the candle and held it over the bowl as she chanted softly.

"Lust will flee." Lizzy opened her eyes and tipped the candle into the water and the flame died with a loud hiss. Picking up the bowl, she offered it to Josh.

"Drink."

"Why?" She looked into his eyes and Josh sensed her disappointment as Lizzy put the bowl back on the bench.

"No matter, just something I wanted to try." She smiled brightly at him and held her hand out as though he hadn't witnessed any of her mumbo jumbo.

"Come to the table, dinner is ready."

Once he had put the little scene in the kitchen out of his mind, he enjoyed the meal and her company. After all, she did believe in ghosts, so what was a little hocus pocus between friends, or even lovers, as his thoughts took a more carnal direction. He was sleeping in the guest room, so he would dig deep into his repertoire of smooth moves and entice her in there with him. Sipping the delicately-flavoured wine, he looked at her beautiful face, satisfied when he saw her staring at his mouth. Putting the glass down, he stood and reached for her hands across the table. She held his gaze as she stood. Her silver hair framed her grey eyes, and if he was any judge, those grey eyes reflected his need. She walked around to him, as though dazed and her lips parted against his. Sliding his hand down her back to draw her close against him, his hardness pushed into her soft belly. His mouth roamed over her soft neck the citrus scent of her hair blending delicately with the apple on his tongue. His teeth grazed her neck and he moved lower, his lips lingering on her nipples through her robe. A shudder went through her body as he reached down, sliding the robe over her head. He gently pushed her away, his gaze feasting on her body. Slender white limbs, covered with two mauve slips of underwear. He slid a gentle finger down her stomach and slipped it inside her briefs, softly stroking. Bending, his mouth followed the trail of his finger and her hands gripped his hair as she gasped.

A low rumble of thunder rolled across the night sky and Lizzy stiffened. His tongue continued its path to heaven. A second louder rumble and the windows shook, and the candles flickered as a gust of wind blew through the open casement. Lizzy stepped back and he saw the regret in her eyes.

***

Lizzy reached for her robe, closing her eyes as the silken fabric fell gently over her near-nakedness, embarrassed by the liberties she had allowed Josh to take. She turned and edged slowly across the room, opening her eyes when she reached the window. Reaching out, she pulled it shut against the storm before she turned and faced Josh across the room. His eyes filled with longing, looked across at her in the candlelight.

Longing, lust…not love. It was a shame he had opened his eyes as she cast her spell. All it had done was doubled both his lust and hers, when the spell had failed.

"We need to sit and talk, Josh." She led him into the living room and he sat on the love seat and patted the empty space next to him. Testing herself and her willpower, she sat close to him.

"There are things you need to know. Things you won't believe." He tipped his head to one side and took her hand in his.

"I want you so much, I will believe anything you want me too," he begged. "I will die if I can't have you."

103

She looked down sadly. "No. Josh, I will die if you have me."

She watched as his head flew up. "That's a strange thing to say. It's the second time you have said that."

She leaned over and kissed him gently on the cheek. It felt like a farewell kiss. "Josh, I know you are a good man. Your Aunt Helen loved you very much and she wanted the best for you." She shook her head gently.

"We have two forces conspiring to push us together. And what I am about to tell you, will decide the future. It depends if you accept or reject what I have to say."

"I don't understand. All I want to do is hold you, love you and make you mine." He frowned at her. "You want that too, I can tell."

"No, you don't really feel that. It is a force beyond you making you feel like that," she said gently. "It is not true love. Do you believe in ghosts, Josh?"

"No." He sighed as he ran his hands through his hair. He looked up at her,

104

confusion on his face. "I don't know…maybe."

"Aunt Helen is trying in her own way to get you to settle in the valley. She wants you to be with me and settle where she thinks you will be happy."

"No freakin' way on earth," he exclaimed. "Three months here is bad enough."

She smiled sadly. "This is going to be the hardest thing for you to understand and accept." She pulled her hair back and leaned forward.

"Look at my neck."

He did as she asked, running his fingers over the pink heart.

"A birthmark?"

"No…" She spoke slowly, wary of his reaction. "The mark of Cupid's arrow." She closed her eyes and waited for the laughter. All was quiet. She opened her eyes as he reached up to his neck, feeling for the mark on his throat. He stood and crossed to the mirror above the fireplace, and leaned forward, squinting in the dim light to examine the mark on his neck. Lizzy held her breath as he sat back down. He leaned forward, his head in his hands.

"Tell me about Cupid's arrow." His voice was expressionless. Lizzy took a deep breath.

"Cupid is the son of Venus, the goddess of love. According to legend, he is often depicted as a mischievous, winged child whose arrows pierce his victims, causing them to fall in love. His name means desire."

"It must be handy, working in the library, knowing all these legends." Josh sounded cynical.

Lizzy ignored him, as the pain ripped through her heart. "According to legend, Cupid's arrows come in two varieties, the golden arrow, which generally signifies true love, and the leaden arrow, which represents wanton and sensual passion." She put her hand on his shoulder, his head turned and he stared away from her into the fire.

"Josh, for some reason that I don't understand, we have both been touched by a leaden arrow. I know when …"

She stopped short as Josh burst out laughing, although there was anger not mirth behind it.

"Oh, for Christ's sake, Lizzy, next you'll be telling me you are a witch and that's what all the hocus pocus in the kitchen was about."

She bowed her head, her hair concealing her face. A gentle rumble of thunder and the hiss of candle wax dripping into the bowl filled the silence.

"If I sleep with you, Josh, I will die…eventually."

Shaking his head in disbelief, he replied. "Yeah, and so will I, one day."

Lizzy took his face in her hands, turning him, to face her. She had to convince him. "Josh, look at me. Pay close attention. Don't be frightened." She took a deep breath and closed her eyes, taking his hand. A whoosh of air came funneling through the room, the candles spluttering until they died. Lizzy held tightly to Josh, as her other hand pointed at the fire and the flames leapt in the hearth. An arc of silver light came from her finger and touched the fire. She pointed at each candle in turn, the flame took hold and the candlelight danced as the candles came alight once more. Josh let go of her hand and jumped to his feet, his eyes wide. Lizzy looked up at him.

"Don't be frightened. It is a natural part of our world." Josh was shaking his head, disbelief written all over his face.

"Now, will you let me try to stop this lust that has its greedy fingers gripping us both?" Josh allowed Lizzy to take his hand and she led him back to the kitchen.

"Josh, I have tried everything tonight. Patchouli, pears, peppermint and radishes. Each of those on their own will dispel lust." She pointed to the stool and he sat, still not speaking a word.

"The problem is, we are not dealing with magic that I am used to. I did some research in the library yesterday." She smiled. "Yes, I do know how to use the internet."

He gave her a rueful grin.

"Legend says that the lust from a leaden arrow will disappear over time. If you help me with a spell, we can beat it down and ease it even more quickly."

"Who says I want it to ease?" he asked. "I have feelings for you, Lizzy."

"Even knowing what I am?" He held her gaze for a moment, doubt crept into his eyes and he dropped his head.

She held her hand out. "Help me, and then we will see what will be. Trust me Josh, and trust your feelings." The candle hissed as the water dripped into the bowl. A fragrance of patchouli and mint passed by him as Lizzy repeated the spell.

"Unwanted crush and lust from thee,

Who drinks this potion will no longer see,

The attraction to his loins desire."

Again, she took a petal from the dead magnolia and placed it in the bowl, held the candle over the bowl as she murmured, "Lust will flee."

Picking up the bowl, she took a sip before offering it to Josh.

"Drink."

Holding her eyes with his, he reached for the bowl.

Chapter 10

The citrus fragrance of Lizzy's shampoo surrounded Josh as he stood under the steaming jets of the shower in the little bathroom off her kitchen. He had slept deeply and dreamlessly and felt refreshed and energised. The pipes creaked as he turned the taps off and stepped out of the shower. Humming a new melody, he closed his eyes and smiled as he thought of the night before. Reaching for a white towel hanging off the door in the pretty bathroom, he draped it around his narrow hips. Stepping to the mirror, he craned forward and examined the small pink heart on the side of his neck.

It was almost gone.

The smell of brewing coffee hastened his dressing and he stepped into the kitchen as Lizzy lifted the coffee pot from the stove.

"Good morning." Her beautiful face lit up in a happy smile.

"You really are one pretty lady." He walked over and dropped a kiss on the top of her head, grinning as she blushed. The sultry witch of the night had gone and Lizzy, the clumsy, shy librarian was back in her place. He wandered over to the window and stared out into the garden, before turning back to her.

"I'm going back to Nashville today, Lizzy."

The distress in her eyes hit him like a sledgehammer. Huge eyes filled with tears, her soft lips were quivering.

"I have to," he said simply.

"I'm sorry I can't love you," she said. "Even though you write me songs, and hold me in your arms as though I am the most beautiful woman in the world." He reached for her and pulled her close.

"It's okay, Lizzy. Don't cry." He smiled at her." It is my choice, nothing to do with you. This valley is not for me, neither is Aunt Helen's farm." He was pleased to see her smile.

"I'm going to give up my inheritance. If I don't take it, the money goes toward the

112

development of a home for elderly folk in the valley." He felt the joy of the last week surround him.

"Maybe Aunt Helen's plan didn't work exactly as she wanted, but I have written a new album and I have made a true friend." He lifted her hand and kissed her palm. Laughing, he continued. "I have also had my eyes opened to a whole new world and I know I have much to learn."

She nodded slowly and a bright smile spread across her face.

"Yes, that is true. Remember me in your songs, Josh, I will be listening."

After they finished their coffee, they stepped outside into the bright morning sunshine and Josh pulled Lizzy into his arms for a final hug. He reached up and tickled her neck where the arrow had marked her and she looked up at him laughing, as the roar of a motorbike drowned out his words. He turned, arms linked around her waist as the warlock stepped off the motorbike, his black hair falling around his face as he removed his helmet.

"Will he turn me into a frog, if I make him jealous?" Josh chuckled as he dipped his head and bravely gave her a final kiss. Stepping into his Porsche, he gave them both a cheery wave and gunned the motor down the driveway. His Porsche was better than the warlock's bike any day.

***

Lizzy stood, arms folded as Wesley strolled over to her.

"Did you have a lovely night, Lizzy?" His voice was sarcastic.

"Wonderful, thank you, Wesley."

"When are you leaving?" Loathing dripped off his words.

"You're the one with the predestination skills, you tell me." Relief quickly turned to anger and her voice rose. She turned on her heel and strode inside to the kitchen. Picking up the crystal goblets and taking them across to the sink, she fought for control, as she ran the glasses under the cold water. It was so good to see him, but by the goddess, she was angry with him.

A warm hand descended on her shoulder and spun her around, the glasses dropping into the sink with a loud clatter. Pushing his hand off, she spoke in a quiet cold voice.

"Don't touch me."

"So, when do you go?"

"What on earth are you on about, Wesley? You're the one who looked into the future, you know everything." Her fingers warmed as she pointed at him and a spark zapped off his shoulder.

"Don't use your magic on me, Lizzy." His voice rose. "One rule for me and one rule for you, you always get to call the shots." He advanced toward her, his arms crossed and a frown wrinkled his beautiful face. She pointed at him, both arms stretched toward him as anger took hold of her body. She smiled nastily as Wesley's feet propelled him backwards and he landed with a thud on the wooden chair at the old scrubbed table. Pushing his hands against the tabletop, he attempted to stand, but she held him in place with the little spell.

115

"You have some explaining to do," she yelled. "Where the hell have you been?"

He looked at her, an evil grin on his face. "Ooh, my quiet little librarian has claws. Oh, goody." Wesley rubbed his hands together. "Lizzy, you forgot there was one little spell you taught me years ago, and I practised and practised."

He flicked a casual finger. Lizzy's feet left the ground, and she landed gently against the cold sink, her back pressing hard on the sharp edge, both feet dangling uselessly a foot above the floor as Wesley's finger held her there casually from the other side of the room. They glared at each other, not speaking. Lizzy fought the bubble of mirth rising from her throat. Her lips twitched and she covered her mouth with one hand, still keeping the other pointed at Wesley. She was determined to remain cross. Looking across the room at that beautiful, familiar face, she saw her mirth reflected in his eyes. He lowered his finger and her feet slid noiselessly to the floor.

"I let you go, now you let me up. Deal?" he asked, his blue eyes twinkling at her.

"I'm still thinking about it," she replied. Cautiously circling the counter top, keeping an eye on him, Lizzy filled the kettle and placed it on the stove.

"I will let you go, if you promise to stay there, while I make fresh coffee." He nodded. As the coffee brewed, she removed two of Mrs. Macpherson's muffins from a container on the table and pushed one across to Wesley. Keeping a wary eye on him, she poured the coffee and sat down across from him. He took a bite and closed his eyes as he chewed. "Mmm, good to be home."

"Where have you been?"

Lazy lids opened slowly and his gaze locked with hers.

"No, Lizzy, you're the one who started this. You do the explaining, not me." He picked the last crumbs off the plate and licked his finger, not taking his eyes from her. Lizzy watched his fingers go to his mouth and a shiver of pure lust shivered through her body.

117

Taken aback, she stared at him, aghast, as her hand reached up and felt around her neck. Her eyes narrowed, and she reached absently for her coffee, concentrating on the warmth pervading her body...and her soul.

"I'm not going anywhere as you well know, Wesley."

"You told your gran you were going to Nashville." His bottom lip dropped in a pout as he returned her stare.

She sighed. "I knew you would go there. I'm disappointed she didn't tell me. Why is everyone on your side?"

Wesley spoke casually. "Because, everyone else knows we are destined to be together." It gave her a great deal of pleasure to see the muscle twitch in his jaw, he wasn't as nonchalant as he was pretending to be.

"And now you have looked, you know what our future holds." Lizzy looked away from him, staring out the window.

Wesley shook his head slowly. "No, I only looked forward one day, the day you sought my bed for the wrong reason." He reached across and held her chin gently, his slender white hand turning her to face him.

"I don't know what will happen. The choice is still yours."

Lizzy held Wesley's intense gaze. "Josh has gone. I reversed the energies. He knows what we are."

"The choice is yours." Wesley smiled at her sadly. "If you ever come to me, it will be for love. I won't accept anything else."

Chapter 11

A week passed by and Lizzy's life slowly returned to normal. She shelved books at the library, and recommended westerns and romances to her elderly patrons. She cleaned out the attic in the cottage, and planted out her winter herbs in the long, sleepy afternoons of the midsummer.

Lizzy kept herself very busy.

Every morning on her way to work, she called in to visit Mrs. Macpherson, collecting the lunchbox for lunch in the park. But, there were no creeping hands on her thigh and no gentle welcoming kisses on her cheek. She tried to kid herself this was how it should be and attempted to get back to enjoying her solitary life, with Wesley as her best friend. He was polite and friendly, but kept a wary distance. Five sleepless nights, despite the best sleeping potion she could brew and Lizzy came to a decision.

On Friday morning, she called into Mrs. Macpherson's cottage. Tapping gently on the front door, she surprised the elderly woman in her nightgown.

"Why, Lizzy, what are you doing here? It's Friday, you don't work at the library today." Her little hands fluttered anxiously. "I can make your lunch, if you have a minute or two to wait?"

Lizzy took Mrs. Macpherson's hands gently between hers.

"Relax, Mrs. Mac. No work today. I called in to ask you a favour."

The old lady breathed a sigh of relief, putting her hand to her head.

"Why, I thought I had mixed my days up. You had me worried my memory was going. Come away in with you, lass. I will make you a nice cup of tea."

Settled at the table in the dining room, crowded with old ornaments and knick-knacks, Lizzy smoothed her hand over the lace crocheted tablecloth.

"Now what's this favour, young lady?"

121

"I was hoping you would ask Wesley to bring something over to me, when he mows your grass this afternoon?"

"Something?" The old lady's face wrinkled in confusion.

"Like bread or muffins, or a pot of herbs. Anything will do." Lizzy cast her gaze down to her hand plucking nervously at the cloth. Looking up again, she surprised a look of absolute delight on the old lady's face. Her eyes were dancing and she clapped her little wrinkled hands together in excitement.

"Oh, is this a plot?" she asked with a little giggle.

"If I ask Wesley to come over, he will know I am up to something." Lizzy smiled at Mrs. Macpherson. "And I do want to surprise him."

Reaching over, the old lady patted Lizzy's arm.

"Leave it with me. I will be delighted to help out."

***

Lizzy was kneeling at her herb garden, her hands in the warm soil, singing quietly to her flowers as Wesley walked around the back of the house, clutching a pot of catnip. Mrs. Macpherson had insisted he take it straight around to Lizzy's cottage before he went home. He was damned if he wanted to go there, it was hard enough having lunch with her every day. The sun was slipping behind Mt. Silverton, and Lizzy did not seem to notice the purple clouds of a summer storm swirling in from the east. Wesley had parked his motorbike out on the road, ready for a quick escape. Walking quietly up her driveway, he intended to leave the pot on her back porch.

His skin glistened with perspiration from mowing the large lawn, and his heart skittered in his chest, uneasy at the thought of coming to Lizzy's cottage. He stood and watched as she planted a row of sweet peas against the trellis at the back of the herb garden. If he hadn't already loved her, he would have fallen for her in that moment. A silver halo shone brightly around her hair, reflected by the setting sun. She stood and as she turned to face him, the slim curves of her body outlined through her sheer gown.

"Not the most sensible gardening clothes." He handed her the catnip. "There's a storm coming too." He snatched his hand away, as she took the herb and ran her fingers lightly up his perspiring arms.

"Catnip from Mrs. Macpherson?" He narrowed his eyes as she smiled sweetly up at him. "How appropriate. Used to captivate your lover and capture his heart forever."

"Expecting the singer back are you, Lizzy?" Wesley asked gruffly as his heart dropped.

"No, Wesley, I'm expecting you. I have made my choice." She looked up at him, eyes shining with love and his world stood still. He stepped forward and said her name and the trees sighed in the wind.

"Lizzy?"

"Yes, Wesley?"

"What are you doing?"

She reached out, took his hand, and led him into her cottage. The smell of lavender and roses drifted across them. Dozens of

124

candles flickered in the soft light and violins shimmered in the soft air. She led him wordlessly upstairs into her bathroom and stood beside a huge bath, filled with steaming water, crushed lavender and rose petals. Still without speaking, she stretched and lifted her silk robe over her head and stood naked before him.

She leaned over and tested the water temperature with her hand, silver hair falling across her face.

"Just right," she smiled and walked over to him. "You need a wash, Wesley."

Lost for words, he allowed her to reach over and undo the snap button on his denim shorts.

She brushed her lips against his chest as she hooked her thumbs in each side of his shorts and dragged them down over his hips.

She smiled as his magnificent arousal sprang out and pushed against her soft skin.

"Not yet, we both need cleansing. She stepped away and lifted one naked slender leg into the fragrant water, holding her hand out for support as she swung her other leg into the water and sat down. The water barely covered her pert little breasts and he watched as the rose petals stuck to her translucent skin. He stepped into the bath and sat opposite her as she spoke.

"I learned to be alone over many years but I loved you from the first day I met you. I loved you as a friend and a brother. You became as essential to me as the air I breathe, and over the years I ignored what you came to mean to me."

His heart was pounding and his love for her was swelling out of his chest. He reached for her and she put up her hand.

"No, hear me out." Her eyes were calm, steady and clear and if he was seeing right, full of love for him. He had waited a hundred years, he could wait another few moments.

"My family could see it, all our dear old friends in the valley could see it." Her beautiful face clouded as she spoke.

"If you had wanted to, you could have looked and you would have known this moment would come. But you loved me so

126

much"—her voice broke and her eyes filled with tears—"you waited and endured the uncertainty of the future." She reached out to him.

"Wesley, I am so sorry I hurt you. I love you, I have always loved you and I will love you for whatever eternity we have. If you will have me, I am yours."

Without answering, he reached over, picking up the soft sponge and wiped the tears from her face. Tears of joy mingled with the beads of moisture on his face.

"No more tears to dim your eyes, you have my heart and soul, forever, my love."

Wesley washed her reverently, and then lay back in the sweet water as Lizzy cleansed the perspiration from his body. He stepped out of the tub and held a warm towel out to her.

When they were dry, she led him into her bedroom and he smiled as he saw the plump cushions and rose petals scattered over the pure white sheets. Dozens of white candles lit the small room and two wine goblets, sat on a silver tray, an uncorked bottle of golden liquid waiting.

"I'm glad you waited for me, Wesley." she smiled up at him.

Epilogue

A fat yellow moon hung heavy in the silver sky as the clock struck midnight and the Beltane holiday began. The strains of a country and western song, plucked on a twelve-string guitar drifted across the moonlit garden and the white flowers nodded with the music. The gathering was intimate. Lizzy's family sat in two rows next to a small fountain, where water bubbled softly over three tiered bowls filled with white flowers. Their elderly friends sat in a row of silk covered chairs next to the herb garden.

"Isn't it most unusual?" Mrs. Macpherson leaned over to old Mrs. McGinty, pointing to the group seated by the fountain. "The whole family has silver hair like Lizzy."

"And how unusual to have country and western music at a wedding," replied Mrs. McGinty. "I thought Lizzy hated country and western music."

Mrs. Macpherson shrugged. "So does Wesley."

Wesley stood alone in the centre of the lawn at the front of a small altar. He stood tall and proud, a white silk shirt billowing loosely over tailored black trousers. A crown of ivy circled his head, his black hair reflecting the moonlight, as he turned and nodded to Josh, sitting above them on the brick steps by the fountain. The notes of Mendelssohn's wedding march drifted softly from the guitar, as both Mrs. Macpherson and Mrs. McGinty pulled out lace-edged handkerchiefs and dabbed at their eyes.

A collective gasp came from the small gathering as twelve white doves swooped from the trees above in the moonlight, dipping in the fountain before perching on the top bowl. Two small children stepped from the cottage and walked slowly along the path to the gathering, strewing white rose petals along behind them.

The music swelled and Lizzy stepped out behind the children, holding the arm of a tall silver haired gentleman, her face covered by a sheer white veil, trailing down her back and across the long train of her silk wedding

130

dress. Her small white slippers followed the trail of rose petals to Wesley and the two old ladies dabbed their eyes once again, as Wesley held his hand out to welcome Lizzy, his eyes glistening with tears of joy.

Lizzy stood next to Wesley and they turned to the altar as their family formed a circle around them. As they plight their troth, acknowledging and paying respect to the beauty of life around them and the powers, a soft murmuring drifted across from the birch tree at the back of the garden.

A young man in a white suit lay back in the tree observing the proceedings below. His bow sat idle next to him. A beautiful woman sat beside him, her legs swinging in the moonlight. A smug smile crossed the young man's face as his mother turned to him.

"Well, my son, the wager has been won. A satisfactory conclusion for all."

"I will be in the Bahamas if you are looking for me, mother." His laugh echoed around the garden as Cupid flew into the silver clouds, his bow trailing behind him.

About the Author

Annie Seaton lives near the beach on the east coast of Australia, fulfilling her lifelong dream of being an author. After majoring in history at university, her career and further study spanned the education sector with the completion of a Masters Degree in Education, and working as an academic research librarian, a high school principal and a university tutor until she took up her full-time writing career. Each winter, Annie and her husband leave the beach to roam the remote areas of Australia for story ideas and research.

Annie's Porter Sisters series is published in print in Australia and New Zealand with Pan Macmillan, and she has recently signed another two book contract with Harper Collins in the Harlequin Mira imprint. *Whitsunday Dawn* is the first of these to be followed by *Undara* in 2019, *Osprey Reef* in 2020 and *East of Alice* in 2021. Annie also has many books published digitally internationally across many genres. You can find them in a convenient slideshow on her website: http://www.annieseaton.net

Readers can contact Annie through her website, http://www.annieseaton.net/ or find her on Face book, Twitter and Instagram.

#1 bestselling author in Amazon Romance series.

Winner ...Book of the Year 2018 AUSROM

Winner ...Best Established Author of the Year 2017 AUSROM

Long listed for the Sisters in Crime Davitt Awards 2016, 2017, 2018.

Finalist in Book of the Year, Long Romance, RWA Ruby awards 2016

Winner ...Best Established Author of the Year 2015 AUSROM

Winner ...Author of the Year 2014 AUSROM

Sign up for Annie's newsletter and stay up to date with her latest news at:

http://www.annieseaton.net/

Most of the books listed below are available in print from Annie's online store at:

http://www.annieseaton.net/store.html

Annie's books

WHITSUNDAY DAWN
UNDARA …July 2019

PORTER SISTERS SERIES
KAKADU SUNSET
DAINTREE
DIAMOND SKY

BONDI BEACH LOVE SERIES
BEACH HOUSE
BEACH MUSIC
BEACH WALK
SORRY WE'RE CLOSED

-

PRICKLE CREEK SERIES
HER OUTBACK COWBOY
HER OUTBACK SURPRISE
HIS OUTBACK NANNY
HIS OUTBACK TEMPTATION

-

SECOND CHANCE BAY SERIES
HER OUTBACK PLAYBOY
HER OUTBACK PROTECTOR
HER OUTBACK HAVEN-April 2019

-

AFFAIRS SERIES
HOLIDAY AFFAIR
ITALIAN AFFAIR
OUTBACK AFFAIR

-

HALF MOON BAY SERIES
TANGLING WITH THE CEO
BRUSHING OFF THE BOSS
GUARDING HIS HEART

LOVE ACROSS TIME SERIES
COME BACK TO ME
FOLLOW ME...Feb 2019

CHRISTMAS WITH THE BOSS
DEADLY SECRETS
ADVENTURES IN TIME
SILVER VALLEY WITCH
CAPTURING THE PIRATE'S
HEART
TEN DAYS IN TUSCANY